Narrator: **Cindy Robinson**

Featuring the voice talents of:

Sofia: **Ariel Winter**
King Roland: **Travis Willingham**
Amber: **Darcy Rose Byrnes**
James: **Zach Callison**
Cedric: **Jess Harnell**
Cinderella: **Jennifer Hale**

Read-Along Executive Producer: Randy Thornton
Read-Along Story Produced by Ted Kryczko and Jeff Sheridan

Based on the movie *Once Upon a Princess*, written by Craig Gerber
Adapted by Lisa Ann Marsoli
Illustrated by Character Building Studio and the Disney Storybook Artists

Read-Along

STORYBOOK AND CD

Once Upon a Princess

Enter the kingdom of Enchancia with Sofia the First
and her new family and friends. You can read along
with me in your book. You'll know it's time to turn
the page when you hear this sound. . . .
Let's begin now.

First Edition
1 3 5 7 9 10 8 6 4 2
ISBN 978-1-4231-9076-9
G942-9090-6-13179

For more Disney Press fun, visit www.disneybooks.com

DISNEP PRESS
New York

Once upon a time, in the kingdom of Enchancia, there lived a little girl named Sofia. She and her mother, Miranda, didn't have much but the cobbler shop, but they were happy.

One morning, Sofia and her mother went to the castle to bring King Roland a new pair of shoes. He and Miranda took one look at each other, and it was love at first sight.

The couple married, and soon Sofia and her mom were off to the castle for a life they never could have imagined.

Miranda lovingly greeted the king's children, Princess Amber and Prince James. Then she gave them each a pin she had embroidered with their family crest. King Roland placed a tiara on Sofia's head. "Welcome to the family!"

"I think it's going to take me a while to get the hang
of things around here."

Amber nodded. "Just follow my lead and you'll be okay."

Sofia was grateful. Her new sister was going to help her learn everything she needed to know—or so she thought!

At dinner that evening, Sofia counted six different forks by her plate! Silverware clattered to the floor as she picked up one fork, then another.

King Roland could see it was going to take a while for Sofia to get used to her new royal life. He had a surprise to help her feel welcome. "We will be throwing a royal ball in your honor at week's end. And you and I shall dance the first waltz."

Later on, Sofia went to her mom's room. "I don't know anything about being a princess. And I don't know how to dance. I'm going to trip, and everyone's going to laugh at me."

Miranda smiled down at Sofia and assured her daughter she'd be fine if she just tried her best.

Just then, they heard a knock at the door. It was King Roland—with a beautiful gift for Sofia!

"It's a very special amulet. So you must
promise to never take it off. Now you best run off to bed.
You have princess school in the morning."

Princess school! Sofia liked the sound of that. Maybe
she could learn how to act like a real princess in time
for the ball after all!

As Sofia skipped back to her room, she bumped into Cedric. The royal sorcerer's beady eyes went straight to the amulet around Sofia's neck.

It was the Amulet of Avalor—the powerful charm Cedric had been trying to get for years! With its magic, he could overthrow King Roland and rule Enchancia. Cedric immediately began to scheme how he'd trick Sofia into giving it to him.

The next morning, Sofia joined Amber and James for the coach ride to Royal Prep Academy. The headmistresses—Flora, Fauna, and Merryweather—greeted her at the gates.

At school, Sofia didn't need to worry about making friends. The other children liked her a lot—which made Amber jealous. She was used to being the popular one!

Amber turned to James. "I think it's time Sofia took a ride on the magic swing."

So James led Sofia to the swing. "Try it! You don't have to kick. It swings itself."

Sofia climbed onto the swing. She was enjoying the ride until the swing sped up and sent her flying into the fountain! Sofia put on a brave smile while the other kids laughed, but James could tell she was upset. He felt terrible about tricking his new sister.

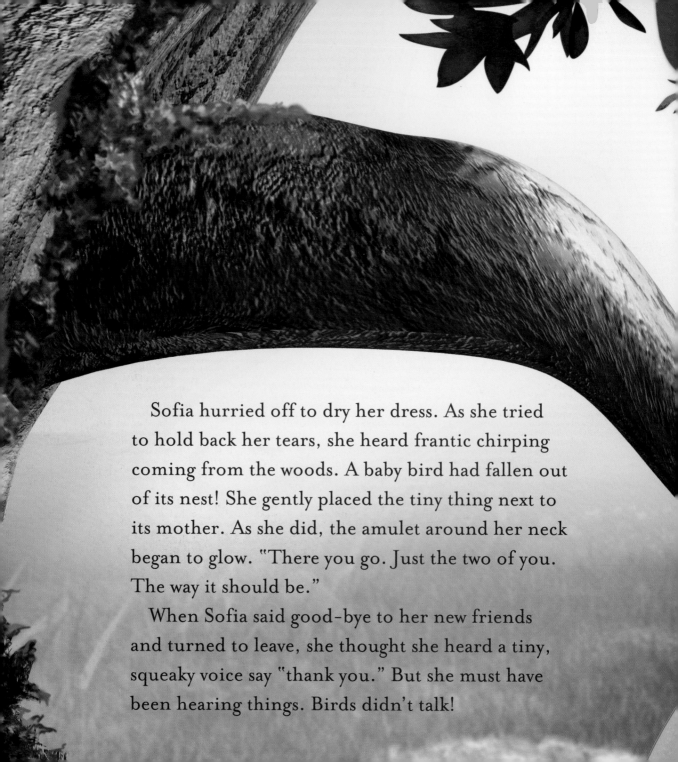

Sofia hurried off to dry her dress. As she tried to hold back her tears, she heard frantic chirping coming from the woods. A baby bird had fallen out of its nest! She gently placed the tiny thing next to its mother. As she did, the amulet around her neck began to glow. "There you go. Just the two of you. The way it should be."

When Sofia said good-bye to her new friends and turned to leave, she thought she heard a tiny, squeaky voice say "thank you." But she must have been hearing things. Birds didn't talk!

When Sofia arrived home from her awful day at school, Cedric was waiting. "How would you like a private tour of my lair—I mean, workshop? Not even the king himself has seen it!"

In Cedric's workshop, Sofia saw a picture of the Amulet of Avalor. "That looks just like my amulet!"

"But if you had the Amulet of Avalor, you'd know. For it contains powerful magic. I can take a quick look at it."

Sofia shook her head. "I promised never to take it off."

As soon as Cedric saw his plan wasn't working, he rushed her out the door. This was going to be tougher than he thought.

The next morning, Sofia awoke to find Clover, a rabbit, and his bird friends Robin and Mia on her bed. They had come to help her get ready—and Sofia could understand every word they were saying! Then she remembered something. "I helped a baby bird yesterday, and I think the amulet gave me the power to talk to animals."

After breakfast with her new friends, Sofia left for Royal Prep. She hoped her second day would be better!

Sofia tried hard in all her classes, but she went home feeling discouraged again. "I thought being a princess would be easy. But it's really hard."

Miranda had a surprise. She led Sofia to the patio, where her two best friends were waiting at a fancy table set for tea. Sofia was so glad to see them! "Jade! Ruby!"

James joined the party, too. He still felt bad about tricking Sofia and wanted to make it up to her.

Soon Sofia was curtsying and pouring tea like a proper princess, but she told James she still didn't know how to dance.

"No problem. We have dance class with Professor Popov tomorrow. You'll be dancing circles around all of us."

Amber had been watching everyone have fun without her. Now she was even more jealous of her stepsister. She had to make sure Sofia didn't dance better than she did.

The next day, before dance class, Amber gave Sofia a sparkling pair of dance slippers to wear.

Sofia put on the slippers, which immediately took control of her feet. She spun helplessly across the floor until the music ended and she collapsed into a pile of pillows.

Amber shrugged. "I must have grabbed a pair of Cedric's trick shoes by mistake. Sorry about that."

Sofia decided she couldn't chance another disaster at the ball—princesses just didn't go crashing into things—so when they got home, she went to Cedric for help.

"I have just the spell for you." He gave Sofia magic words to say when the waltz began. Little did she know that the spell would put everyone to sleep and help Cedric steal the amulet!

Soon it was time to get ready for the ball. Amber was
admiring herself in the mirror when James came in.

"You gave Sofia the trick shoes on purpose. You're trying
to ruin her ball because everyone likes her more than you.
And after what you did today, so do I!"

"James! Come back!" Amber went after him—and
accidentally tore her gown! How could she go to the ball now?

Sofia stood in front of her own mirror and stared at herself in her fancy gown and glittering tiara. She felt like a real princess!

For the first time that week, Sofia was actually looking forward to the ball!

A little while later, everyone watched as King Roland
proudly escorted a beaming Sofia into the ballroom.
The orchestra began to play. It was time for the first waltz!

Sofia confidently spoke the magic words Cedric had given
her: "Somnibus populi cella."

Everyone instantly fell asleep—including Cedric!

"I must have said it wrong!" Sofia ran out of the ballroom. It seemed as if ever since she had become a princess, she couldn't do anything right. Sofia sank to the floor and cried. A single tear fell onto her amulet and made it glow. Suddenly, a blue light appeared—and transformed into Cinderella!

"Your amulet brought me here. It links all the princesses that ever were. And when one of us is in trouble, another will come to help. Why are you so sad, Sofia?"

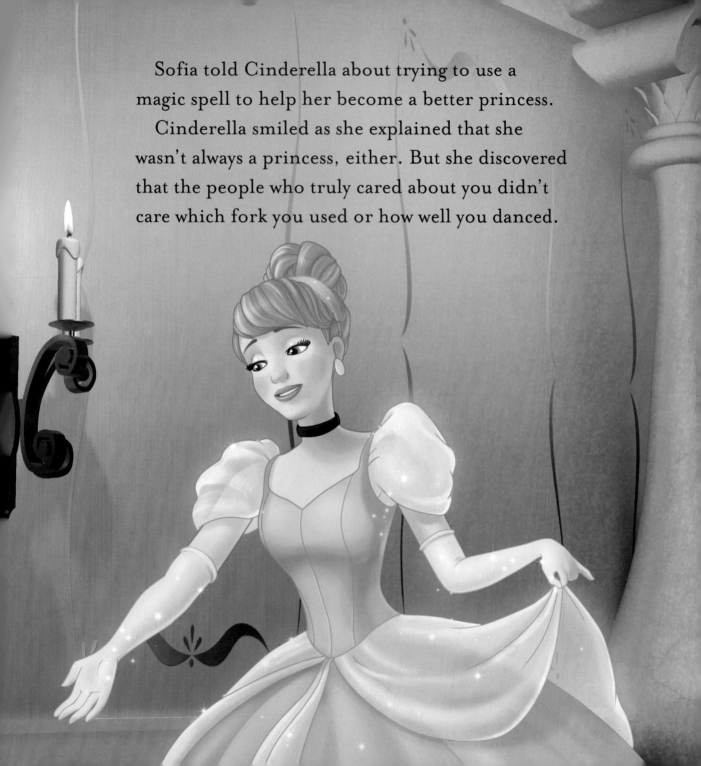

Sofia told Cinderella about trying to use a magic spell to help her become a better princess. Cinderella smiled as she explained that she wasn't always a princess, either. But she discovered that the people who truly cared about you didn't care which fork you used or how well you danced.

Cinderella couldn't undo the spell, but she suggested that
Sofia try to become true sisters with Amber—something she'd
never been able to do with her own stepsisters. "Perhaps all
she needs is a second chance." Then Cinderella disappeared!

Sofia went to Amber's room. "I've done something terrible."
She told her stepsister about the spell and then led her to the
ballroom. When Amber saw her father, she gasped in shock!

Sofia felt terrible. "It's all my fault."

Amber shook her head. "No, Sofia. You wouldn't have
needed the spell if I didn't give you those trick shoes."

The girls realized that what they really needed was each other.

Together they went to Cedric's workshop to find a spell to
wake everyone up—but they had to get past Cedric's pet raven,
Wormwood, first. Clover, Mia, and Robin helped, and soon the
raven was locked in his cage. "Let's find that counterspell!"

Wormwood didn't realize that with her amulet, Sofia could
understand every word he said. So Clover tricked him into
revealing where the counterspell book was hidden.

Now Cedric's spell could be broken!

Sofia and Amber were rushing to the ballroom when Amber remembered her torn dress. "I can't go in there looking like this."

But Sofia wasn't about to leave her sister behind. She quickly mended the gown. "There you go. Good as new!"

Now it was Amber's turn to help. She led her sister in a waltz until Sofia was ready for the ball.

Sofia smiled as she took her place beside the king. "Populi cella excitate!" To her relief, everyone woke up.

Cedric was furious that his plan had been ruined!
He flicked his wand and disappeared in a puff of smoke.
"Merlin's mushrooms!"

Meanwhile, Sofia and the king began to waltz.

Sofia looked up at her new dad. "I've been wondering. Why do they call you Roland the Second?"

The king explained to Sofia that his father had also been named Roland.

"So I guess that makes me Sofia the First."

And it was plain to see that this princess was going to live happily ever after!